Boo! Who?

Colin and Jacqui Hawkins

Holt, Rinehart and Winston
New York

Who's there, in the chair?

Ding, dong, don't be long.

Open wide and see inside.

Fiddle-de-de, who can you see?

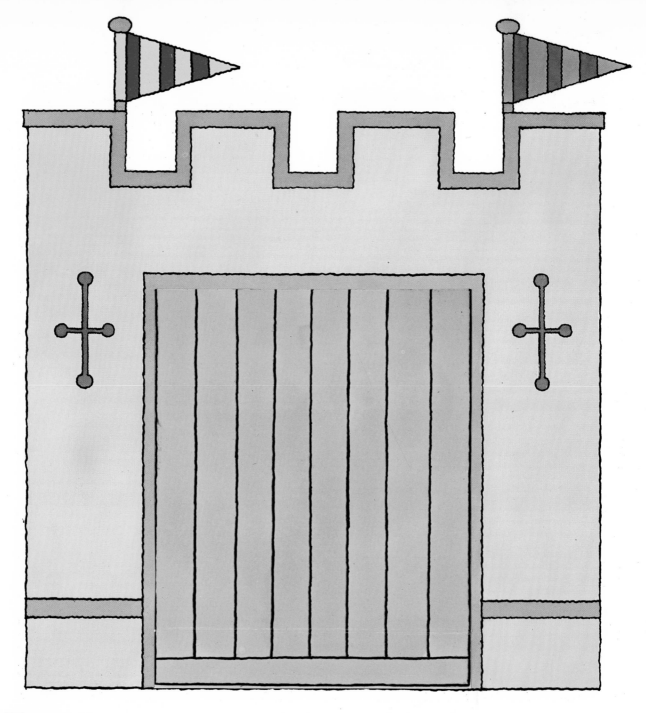

Rat-a-tat-tat, who is that?

Who's in the house, is it a mouse?

Who should not be in the cot?

Take a peep and see who's asleep.

One, two, three, look and see.

Munch, munch, who's having lunch?

Rub-a-dub-dub, who's having a scrub?

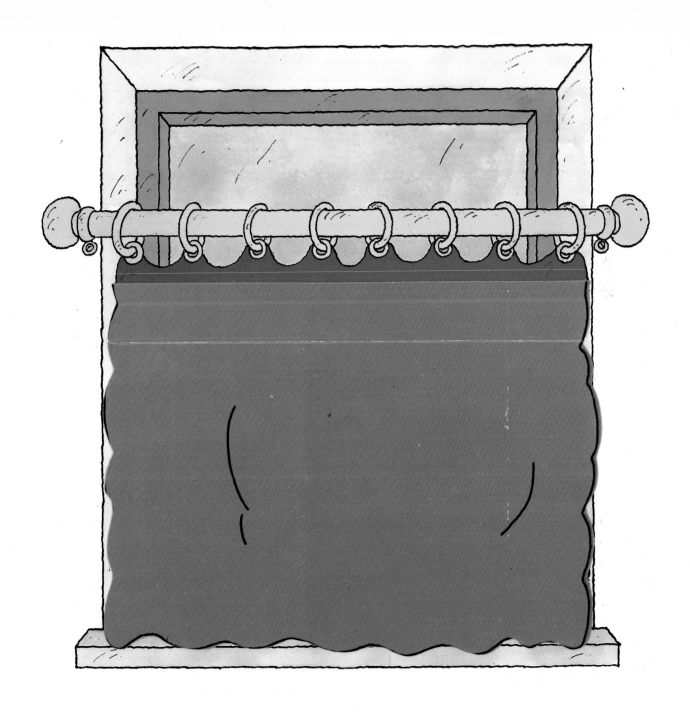

Who's that, is he very fat?

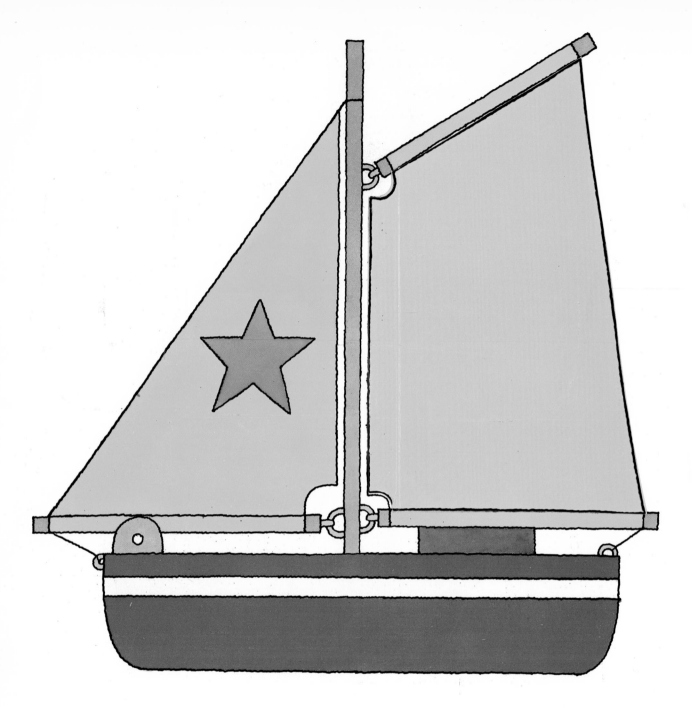

Lift the sail, do you see a whale?

Snug inside, who's trying to hide?